# princess
## Kai-lan

adapted by Diana Michaels

based on the screenplay written by Chris Nee and Sascha Paladino

illustrated by Kellee Riley

Ready-to-Read

SIMON SPOTLIGHT/NICKELODEON

New York    London    Toronto    Sydney

Based on the TV series *Ni Hao, Kai-lan!*™ as seen on Nick Jr.™

SIMON SPOTLIGHT/NICKELODEON
An imprint of Simon & Schuster Children's Publishing Division
1230 Avenue of the Americas, New York, New York 10020
© 2010 Viacom International Inc. All Rights Reserved. NICKELODEON, *Ni Hao, Kai-lan!*,
and all related titles, logos and characters are trademarks of Viacom International Inc.
All rights reserved, including the right of reproduction in whole or in part in any form.
SIMON SPOTLIGHT, READY-TO-READ, and colophon are registered trademarks of Simon & Schuster, Inc.
For information about special discounts for bulk purchases, please contact Simon & Schuster Special Sales at
1-866-506-1949 or business@simonandschuster.com.
Manufactured in the United States of America 0711 LAK
4  6  8  10  9  7  5  3
ISBN 978-1-4424-0351-2

I am Kai-lan.

I am playing butterfly ball
with my friends.

Look! Something in the air
is flying this way!

Look! It landed near a tree.

It is the Monkey King!

He needs our help.

He will use his magic stick

to show us what is wrong.

"A wall divides the two kingdoms in the Land of Foxes and Bears. The Foxes and the Bears are not friends," says the Monkey King.

The Monkey King needs
our help to show the Bears
and the Foxes
how to be friends.
We can help the Monkey
King.
Friends always help friends!

Jump!
We jump onto clouds that
take us to the Land of
Foxes and Bears.

We made it to the Land of
Foxes and Bears!
A baby bear looks through
a little hole in the wall!
"My name is Tian Tian,"
says the baby bear.

Then a baby fox says hello.

"I am Xin Xin," he says.

"Would you like a peach?"

I want a peach! So do Hoho,

Tolee, and Rintoo!

"I want a peach too, Kai-lan!" says Tian Tian.

"Can you ask the baby fox for me? Bears do not speak to Foxes."

I ask Tian Tian to try.

The baby fox gives a peach
to the baby bear!
Now they are friends!
If the Bear Queen and Fox
King talk, maybe they could
be friends too!

First we will talk
to the Fox King.
Do you see his castle?

The castle doors are locked.

We will find a way

to sneak inside!

Be very quiet!

The Fox King does not want to talk to us.

But I have a present for him.

I brought him a peach.

The Fox King likes the peach.

Now he will talk to us!

He explains why the Foxes

and the Bears are not friends.

"We are not friends with the Bears because they make the ground shake when they dance," says the Fox King. "The shaking makes us mad."

The Foxes never told the Bears why they are mad. So the Bears might not know! We must talk to the Bear Queen.

"Why are the Bears mad at the Foxes?" we ask the Bear Queen.

"Their singing is too loud," says the Bear Queen.

"It makes us mad."

I know how we can help!
When you feel mad,
talk about what is making
you mad, so your friends
can help you like good
friends do!

The Fox King and the Bear
Queen talk to each other!
If they talk about what is
wrong, maybe they can
become friends!

"Oh! We did not know our dancing makes you angry," says the Bear Queen.
"And we did not know our singing bothers you," says the Fox King. "We are sorry."

The Bear Queen says,
"The Bears can dance
and the Foxes can sing at
the same time!
We will all be friends and
play together!"

So the Foxes start singing,

and the Bears start dancing.

It is a party!

They are all friends!

The Fox King and Bear
Queen say, "We will take
down the wall, and make
this a Kingdom of Friends.
Kai-lan will be our princess!
Princess Kai-lan!
Princess of Friends!"